S0-AFM-988

KNOCK KNOCK

KNOCK
KNOCK
KNOCK

KNOCK KNOCK KNOCK

KNOCK

KNOCK

TAMMI SAUER GUY FRANCIS

KNOCK KNOCK

For Janee, Jessica, and Kim — T.S.
In loving memory of my mom, Ann Francis — G.F.

Text copyright © 2018 by Tammi Sauer • Artwork copyright © 2018 by Guy Francis
All rights reserved. Published by Scholastic Inc., *Publishers since 1920.* SCHOLASTIC and associated logos are trademarks and/or registered trademarks of Scholastic Inc. The publisher does not have any control over and does not assume any responsibility for author or third-party websites or their content. • No part of this publication may be reproduced, stored in a retrieval system, or transmitted in any form or by any means, electronic, mechanical, photocopying, recording, or otherwise, without written permission of the publisher. For information regarding permission, write to Scholastic Inc., Attention: Permissions Department, 557 Broadway, New York, NY 10012. • This book is a work of fiction. Names, characters, places, and incidents are either the product of the author's imagination or are used fictitiously, and any resemblance to actual persons, living or dead, business establishments, events, or locales is entirely coincidental. • ISBN 978-1-338-31593-6 • 10 9 8 7 6 5 4 3 2 1 18 19 20 21 22
Printed in the U.S.A. 169 • First printing 2018 • Book design by Steve Ponzo

Scholastic Inc.

KNOCK KNOCK

Who's there?
Justin.
Justin who?

Justin the neighborhood and thought I'd stop by!

KNOCK KNOCK
Who's there?
Ken.
Ken who?

Ken you let us in already?

Oh, boy.

KNOCK KNOCK
BEE

Who's there?
Luke.
Luke who?
Luke out! Here I come!

KNOCK KNOCK
Who's there?
Olive.
Olive who?

Olive us!

Good grief.
KN

OCK KNOCK
Who's there?
Ima.
Ima who?
Ima gonna huff and puff and blow the house down if you don't open this door!

Doesn't anybody see that I need to get some . . . *yawwwwnnn.*

KNOCK KNOCK
KNOCK KNOCK
KNOCK KNOCK

WHO'S THERE?

Al.
Al who?

Al miss you all winter long.

HAPPY HIBERNATION

Awww. I'll miss you guys, too!

Sleep well.
Sweet dreams.

Goldilocks
See you in spring.

ZZZZZZZ

ZZZZZZ

Three months later . . .

SPRING

KNOCK KNOCK
Who's there?
Harry.
Harry who?
WELCOME

Harry up!
It's spring!

KNOCK KNOCK
KNOCK KNOCK
KNOCK KNOCK
KNOCK KNOCK
KNOCK KNOCK
KNOCK KNOCK
KNOCK KNOCK
KNOCK KNOCK
KNOCK KNOCK